MW00938619

THE DARKNESS IN THE SHADOW

THE HAUNTING OF BRIAR PARK

CARRIE KING

CAROLINE CLARK

CAZCLARK.COM

THE HAUNTING OF BRIAR PARK

I first wrote the Briar Park books some years ago. I was told the story by one of my friends! Well he was until he scared me to death and had me sleeping with the light on for the next week.

Briar Park wouldn't leave me alone and I knew I had to write it all down and soon characters were coming into my mind. They wanted to visit the Park... little did they know.

So I wanted to write and publish the books but how should I do it? As a gal from New York who loves all that is Spooky but knows nothing about the internet this was not easy.

I so wanted to share these stories and have been trying to get them published for some time. That's not too easy for a gal from New York who knows very little about anything but my black cat, Samantha, books, and yes you got it creepy houses.

Well I had a go at putting the books up on Amazon and then went on a ghost hunting trip to the United Kingdom. There I met another author Caroline Clark and we got talking.

Caroline is a very successful author and she liked my books. Woo Hoo.

So she offered to work with me to improve them and bring them under her publishing umbrella. So there you have it. This book has been rewritten and edited and I hope you will enjoy the creepy spookiness of two very dark ladies.

This is the 4th book in The Haunting of Briar Park Series. Though each can be read alone I think you will enjoy them all the more if you read them in order. They are all free on Kindle Unlimited or just 0.99 to own.

Something Evil This Way Comes

With Wicked Intent

Silent Screaming

The Darkness in the Shadow

Enjoy,

Carrie King.

he House in Briar Park – Book 4

The Darkness in the Shadows

England, 1990

Clouds of dust billowed into the air and the constant noise and drone of heavy equipment rumbled over the site embedded deep in the woods. Men in high-vis vests scurried around, their faces glum. They were all intent on finishing their tasks on time, to schedule, and with the minimum of fuss. Not one of them wanted this job to continue into another week.

The crack of metal machinery connecting with, and breaking through, live tree trunks blended with the roar of diesel motors and, here and there, the shout of a supervisor overseeing and instructing his crew.

Roger pushed his hard hat back a little in order to scratch at the sparse and sweat-drenched hair on his head. He turned to Frank, his off-sider for the duration of this project.

"This has turned into more of a nightmare than I'd ever imagined. We're days behind."

Frank, a burly man with heavily tattooed arms, folded together the large sheet of plans he'd been studying and nodded. He smiled a little, Roger was the only man on site who didn't swear and sometimes it amused him.

"I know. It seems we've dealt with one delay after another, and the whole thing has been a bloody nightmare. But I'm hoping we're past the worst of it. If all goes well, we should be done by nightfall tomorrow."

"Hey!"

A piercing shout could be heard above the sound of

the machinery. It was followed by a pause in the movement from one side of the construction, where a small crew of men labored over the removal of a small stand of sycamore trees.

Frank and Roger looked over in the direction of the commotion. Moments later, a sickening scream tore through the air. The two men looked at each other for a moment, then ran toward the source of the disturbance.

"What is it?" Roger was puffing and slightly out of breath by the time he'd covered the short distance to where the earthmover now stood idle.

Several white-faced men were standing and staring down at something which lay at their feet. He couldn't quite make it out but there was something disturbing about the whole scene.

Tony, the supervisor, whirled around. His face was deathly pale. "Call the paramedics. It's John. And it looks bad."

Frank arrived at the scene, a few steps behind Roger. The two men looked down at the bundle of clothes before them and it was a few moments before the scene sunk in. It wasn't just clothes but skin, and gore, what was left of a man lay at the center of the small circle of men.

Frank was already reaching for his mobile phone. He lifted the device to stab in the emergency number when he suddenly doubled over and turned away, vomiting copiously on the turned-over ground.

Roger swallowed hard as he made out the name tag. John, a genial father-of-two and a favorite with his workmates, lay in a broken heap on the soil. Roger was no doctor, but even he could clearly see that it was too late for the paramedics. John's body was twisted in an impossible knot, his arms broken and lying at old angles behind his head, his legs snapped at the knees and pointing in opposite directions. A large portion of his face was missing.

"How did this happen?" Roger whispered as bile rose in the back of his throat.

He could hear Frank, now recovering slightly, talking urgently into the phone behind him. Several of the work crew were sobbing quietly. One of the young men stumbled away, falling to his knees in the dirt.

Tony shook his head. He looked as if he was about to faint.

"No one saw what happened. John had just walked into the trees to check for any major obstacles before the earthmover went in. The next minute he was ... he was thrown out of the woods and onto the ground at our feet. Like this."

Tony swallowed hard and looked across at his men. They were nodding in agreement, their faces twisted in horror.

Roger frowned. "What do you mean, he was thrown out of the woods? That makes no sense at all." Obviously, the machine driver must have not seen the man and run him over... only surely... even the earth mover wouldn't make such a mangled mess.

Tony looked at him solemnly. His Adam's apple was bobbing rapidly up and down.

"I know it makes no sense. But we all saw it with our own eyes."

Roger felt a shudder pass over him as the clouds covered the sun. There had been something oppressive about this site since the moment they walked on, but this had to be an accident... didn't it?

2

*G*erald banged his hand down on the desk. His pen jumped a few inches in the air, then rolled across the oak desktop. He glared at Roger.

"This is a catastrophe! This project has gone weeks over schedule and thousands of pounds over budget. The health and safety record of the whole company has been blighted with one incident after another and now this... you've got some explaining to do. The Briar Park development has been the worst disaster in our company's records." Gerald's face was red, his eyes wide and his adam's apple bounced in his throat.

Roger took a deep breath. He knew the responsibility

stopped with him. What had happened was on his shoulders, and he was prepared to accept the consequences. He stared at his boss. He'd never seen Gerald so fired up, and he couldn't blame him. The site had been closed for inspection by the health and safety executive following John's terrible death. Roger had never had a death on his construction and he prided himself on keeping his men safe and yet only a matter of days after they'd been cleared to return to work, another worker, Billy had been involved in an awful accident.

Billy was still alive, barely, but the doctors had warned that he might never regain consciousness. Roger swallowed the lump that threatened to choke him. He almost hoped that the man didn't recover, given the extent of his injuries.

Roger leaned forward slightly. "I'm not trying to make excuses, but even the health and safety crew were unable to determine what had happened to John. No one saw it—he was out of sight in the trees. The best they could come up with was that some kind of wild animal got hold of him."

Gerald puffed his cheeks out. His face was red. "Really! I find that very hard to believe. Wild

CARRIE KING & CAROLINE CLARK

animals in England, so you think a squirrel or a rabbit could do that to a man?"

Roger shook his head, it made no sense, but what else could it be? Maybe there was an escaped zoo animal or a serial killer lurking in the woods... there seemed to be no other explanation. "And Billy ..." He trailed off, remembering. He shut his eyes for a moment, then opened again to look squarely at Gerald. "What happened to Billy *could not* have happened."

Gerald rolled his eyes in exasperation.

"What a ridiculous thing to say, since it *has* happened! Roger, this is your responsibility. You were in charge of the entire site. We have one man dead and another in the hospital, fighting for his life, with injuries no man should have ever have sustained. Roger, the medical professionals say that his entire scrotum was ripped from his body. Can you imagine such a thing?" Gerald shuddered. "This can't get out. As far as the public need to know, this was an unfortunate industrial accident, nothing more."

Both men stared at each other and swallowed hard. The extent of Billy's injury was incomprehensible.

And, as Roger knew, the investigation had so far revealed no cause for the shocking event. Billy's accident had once again occurred out of sight of the other men working at Briar Park.

Roger cleared his throat.

"Billy was in the same area as John was when his accident happened. He'd spoken to Tony, the supervisor, only moments before. Everything seemed to be fine. Tony has filled out an incident report, and as he has stated already, he knows nothing more than that Billy was going back into the trees to collect the tools. The other men had mostly clocked off for the day. Evening was falling, and it was just a matter of tidying the site for the night. I was over at the office completing the last of the paperwork when Tony ran over to get me. He swears he saw or heard nothing until Billy screamed."

There was a sudden urgent banging on the office door. Both men turned as the door was flung open heavily, bouncing off the wall behind it.

Annabel, Gerald's PA, was standing in the doorway. She looked as if she was about to collapse.

"Mr. Seibel? There's been another accident."

9

3

William drove the car through the well laid out streets of the Briar Park housing estate. On every lot a partially completed or recently finished new house stood. The gardens were in the final stages of landscaping, and street lights marched proudly along the borders of the neat little roads.

Briar Park had been a very popular new development from the day it first opened for sale, and the lots had sold quickly.

William pulled the car over to the curb and switched off the engine. He bent his head a little to stare through the windscreen at the house now standing before them.

"I love it, darling."

Sandra reached over from the passenger seat and squeezed her husband's leg gently. She gazed at the house for several minutes before looking back at him, her face radiant.

"It's just perfect."

William smiled at his pretty young wife. With her blonde hair and heart-shaped face she always made him want to smile, to sing and to shout out how lucky he was. Then he looked back at the house. He had wanted to purchase one of the new dwellings in the development, but as soon as Sandra had seen the original house, a property built in the 1700s which still stood in the middle of the parcel of land, she had wanted no other. She had begged and pleaded with him to buy the house, and finally he had given in. All he could see when he looked at the old two-story house was hard work and renovations, but Sandra had seen glimpses of happiness and joy within its aged walls.

"Let's go inside! I'm so excited. Do you have a key?" Sandra had already opened the car door and placed one foot on the curb.

William grinned and undid his seatbelt. "Of course. Do you want me to carry you over the threshold?"

Sandra blew a kiss in his direction from where she stood on the street, before shutting the car door with a bang.

William climbed out of the car and leaned against the car for a minute, staring at the house. Was he imagining it, or was there a cloud of yellow dust hanging in the air above the property?

He looked around.

There was a lot of construction work still going on in the area. No doubt a lot of dust would be stirred up for quite some time to come.

He walked over to join Sandra on the front step.

Sandra slipped her arm through William's as he placed the key in the lock. He pushed the door open, picked her up, and carried her over the threshold, both of them laughing and giggling as they made their way inside.

William put her down and stole a quick kiss.

Sandra sighed up at him and pulled back. Before

she completely moved away she impulsively threw her arms around his neck, covering his face with kisses.

"Thank you," she cried. "Thank you for buying this house for me."

William put his arms around Sandra's waist and held her close. "I just want you to be happy," he said.

He kissed the top of her head.

"But we have a lot of work to do, darling, and a lot of cleaning, too. Look at the dust!" He dropped his arms and walked over to the banister of the stairs, dragging his finger through the thick yellow dust that blanketed the wood.

"I don't care." Sandra spun around in a happy circle. "This house is perfect."

She turned away from the entrance way and walked into the kitchen.

"I love this kitchen. The old wood stove is still here. It adds so much character! And the room is so bright with all these windows." She walked to the end of the room and rubbed her hand across the dusty window to clear a space. "And look, we have three sycamore trees on our property. I'm so glad the developers left them there."

William walked over to join Sandra. He felt a sneeze building in the back of his nose. The dust in the house was appalling and floated up as they moved.

He used the sleeve of his jacket to clear more of a space on the window pane. The three sycamore trees bordered the property, set up close to the new fence which marked their boundary.

"What's that?" he pointed.

"What, where?" Sandra stood on tiptoes to try and see what William was looking at.

"I think it's an old pump, or maybe an artesian well. I didn't notice it before when we viewed the place. I'm going outside to take a look. Do you want to come?"

Sandra shook her head. "No, I want to look around inside. I'm so excited. William, we're going to make a wonderful new beginning in this house."

She looked at her husband seriously for a moment. "I'm sure this marks a change for us. Perhaps once we're settled in …"

She gazed up at him, the pain evident in her blue eyes.

William ducked his head and kissed her forehead. "Another baby will come. Give it time. You've got enough to think of for now. You're going to be so busy, you'll barely have a moment to think or worry." He patted her rump gently. "I'll just go and check on the garden."

Sandra turned away and began opening and closing cupboards.

William reached the doorway and looked back.

"The delivery company will bring the furniture in the morning. Are you sure you want to stay here tonight? It won't be too comfortable sleeping on the floor. I can still find us a hotel."

Sandra shook her head firmly. "No, I want to stay here. This is our house now, and I'm never leaving."

William laughed. "After months of renovations, you might wish you'd never arrived! Don't be too quick to say that you're never leaving."

He walked down the short hallway toward the back door. He tried the door leading to the basement as he passed it. The real estate agent had not had a key to the downstairs room when he'd shown the couple the property, but he had promised to send a locksmith to the house. The door was still firmly locked. Whistling, William stepped into the living room. There against the wall was a painting of a forest with a monk working in a garden. Next to him there was a rip in the canvas. That would have to go.

Picking up the picture he went to the back door and stepped down into the garden, tossing the broken painting into the bin.

William stood beside the house and looked around. Their property was still of a reasonable size. The garden was much bigger than the new build properties that surrounded them, but nothing remotely close to the area the original grounds had covered.

The couple had been told a brief history of the house, from the time it was first built in the 1700s. The estate agent had told them it had belonged to a local monastery for a period of time, and since then a range of owners had passed through its doors.

Sandra had been enchanted at the thought of owning

such an old property, and she had fallen in love with it in moments. He still had his doubts though, sometimes looking at it made his skin crawl... but he would put his own doubts aside. Sandra deserved some joy and he would make sure she got it.

He looked over towards a pile of wood heaped against the side of the house. The woodstove in the kitchen still worked, apparently, and there was a fireplace in the living room. William was fond of a good open fire. In his opinion, there was nothing better than relaxing beside a roaring fire on a cold winter's night, a glass of red wine in hand and the beautiful woman he loved by his side. He smiled at the thought. It was good to see Sandra so happy again.

It was a lovely day and he felt the sun on his back as he walked over to the pump he'd noticed from the window. Weeds grew and twisted through the aged mechanism, and rust covered most of it. He squatted down, pulling the weeds aside, and gave the pump an experimental push. The rusted metal gave slightly under the pressure of his hand, but then stopped. It was probably years since it had been used.

He looked around and spotted a sturdy stick lying in

the grass close by. Getting up, he walked over to pick it up. Perhaps if he leveraged the wood under the pump handle, he could break through the decades of rust and loosen it a little.

William looked up from his task a moment later, frowning. What was that sound?

There was nothing that he could see but a whispering or a muttering was coming from nearby? Whatever it was, it was urgent and intense and very disconcerting. He stared around. The leaves of the sycamore trees rustled in the breeze. Suddenly, a piercing scream reached his ears. Sandra! He dropped the stick and sprinted towards the house, his heart pounding.

4

William threw the door back against its hinges and ran inside the house. "Sandra!" he called frantically. "Where are you? Are you all right?" His mouth was dry, and he could hear his own heartbeat in his ears.

"I'm up here. I'm okay," Sandra's voice drifted down the stairs.

William took the stairs two at a time. "What happened? I heard you scream from out in the garden."

Sandra was standing in the doorway to the bathroom, her arms wrapped around herself in a hug.

"I'm sorry. I didn't mean to scare you. Look."

With a shaking finger, she pointed at the old claw-footed tub standing in the middle of a maze of black and white floor tiles.

William followed her gaze. He stared for a moment, then burst into laughter.

"It's just a spider! Jesus, I thought you'd been murdered."

In a few steps, he stood in front of the bathtub.

"Poor little thing; it's probably terrified."

He reached down to pick up the insect, intent on opening the bathroom window and placing it on the ledge outside.

"Shit!"

He recoiled quickly and stood up, looking at his finger. "It bit me."

"I told you that all spiders are evil."

Sandra spoke from the doorway, but she made no attempt to come any closer. "Don't try and save it.

Kill it. Squash it," her voice rose and was slightly hysterical.

William sucked at his finger. He'd never experienced a spider bite, and he had not expected to feel such pain from such a tiny creature. Already, the tip of his finger was throbbing. The spider moved suddenly, scurrying quickly across the white ceramic surface in a flurry of long, scrabbly legs. He raised his foot and stomped his boot down into the tub, leaving the insect with no chance of survival.

He heard Sandra let out a sigh of relief behind him as he removed his foot from the tub and stared at the smeared remains of the creature with satisfaction.

"Maybe we should get the pest control people in," Sandra said. "This place must be crawling with bugs." She shuddered.

"It might be a good idea." William looked at his finger again. He could clearly see two small puncture wounds on the tip, and the surrounding area of skin was red. His flesh still throbbed with pain.

"I hope that spider wasn't poisonous. It managed to take a sizable bite out of my finger."

He shook his hand quickly and turned back to Sandra.

"Come on. We'll go and get our things out of the car and set up the beds."

WILLIAM SMILED as he drove back into the estate, the headlights of the car picking up their neighbors' properties as he turned into their street.

Sandra was still giggling beside him, highly amused by the joke he had just made.

He pulled the car over and switched off the engine.

"Well, I guess it does bode well that we've discovered a good local restaurant nearby already. I can see Mrs. Chang's fine establishment becoming a firm favorite for future evenings out. Now we've been fed and watered are you ready for our first night in our new house?"

He flicked off the car lights.

"William, what is that? It looks like there's a light coming from the upstairs window."

Sandra turned back to him, her face creased into a frown.

"I'm sure we didn't leave any lights on."

William felt the faint stirrings of apprehension. He too was sure that no lights had been left on.

"Wait here," he said firmly. "I'll go and check. I'm sure it's nothing."

He walked toward the house, feeling uneasy. He'd locked the front door when they'd left; he was positive of that, but had he locked the back door? He pushed the door key into the lock, noticing the throb and ache of the spider bite as he did so. Nudging the front door open, he stepped cautiously inside onto the wide floorboards of the entranceway.

"Hello?"

His voice echoed back at him from the white painted walls of the empty house. He flicked on the light switch beside the door, flooding the entrance way with welcome light. He glanced back at the car. Sandra was now leaning against the side of the vehicle, watching him.

"Hello?" he called again, and stopped and listened.

The house answered with a slight creak, but nothing more. William glanced into the empty kitchen and living room as he passed, and then he began to climb the stairs. The wound on his finger prickled and burned.

He reached the upper landing and turned on the light. From outside, the light appeared to be coming from the second bedroom. But from here the room was dark.

He walked quickly into the room, which was cloaked in thick darkness.

Running his hand over the cold wall, he switched on the light. A quick movement in one corner caught his eye, and he whirled around.

The room was bare and empty, except for a slight haze of yellow dust which hung in the air. The strange whispering noise he'd heard earlier started again, then stopped just as abruptly.

William turned around in the room. There was nothing there, nowhere to hide and then a tree branch scrapped across the window.

Letting out the breath he hadn't been aware he was

holding, William turned to walk back downstairs again. It was just the wind whispering in the trees. The light must have just been a reflection from one of the neighboring properties.

He had reached the kitchen doorway when Sandra suddenly walked out of the darkness of the room, startling him.

"Jesus, Sandra! I thought I told you to wait outside."

His heart was pounding uncomfortably, and the bite on his finger throbbed harder in response to his agitation. His voice was harsher than he meant it to be.

"Sorry, I didn't mean to frighten you. I was looking at the window and I realized that the light was a reflection from one of the street lights. There was nothing upstairs, was there?"

Sandra moved forward to wrap her arms around her husband.

He shook his head but something didn't feel right.

"Awww, William, were you spooked?" she teased.

"Don't." William pushed Sandra's arms away abruptly.

She stepped back and looked at him in hurt surprise. "William?"

He shook his head.

"I'm sorry. I didn't mean to be short with you. I'm just tired, I guess. And that stupid spider bite still hurts."

He held his finger out and the couple studied the wound in the light of the entrance way. A faint shimmer of pus seeped from the puncture marks, and the skin around them was red and inflamed.

"I think you'd better get that looked at," Sandra said, peering closely at the injury. "It looks infected."

"I'll be fine for now. I'll rinse it in a little antiseptic because I'm not going out again tonight. This is nothing." He waved the offending digit trying to ignore the pain. "I can just about guarantee it'll be back to normal by the morning anyway. Do we still have that old first aid box in the car? Perhaps I'll put a plaster on it as well." William had already turned back to the front door.

Sandra nodded. "Yes, it's under the passenger seat." She flipped on the kitchen light. "I'm making a hot drink. Do you want one?"

"Yes, I'll have tea, please. I'll get the kit from the car."

William walked back out the front door. A chill breeze whipped around him, and leaves swirled across the pathway in front of him as he covered the short distance to the car.

He opened the door and bent down to retrieve the first aid box. Once he found it he shut the car door again, locking it behind him, and glanced back up at the upstairs window. It *did* look as though there was a light on up there. He stared around, trying to see the street light that Sandra had said was reflected in the pane.

A sudden cackling laugh sprang at him from out of the darkness and he turned around quickly, peering down the street.

Heart beating fast he could see the road was empty.

The breeze picked up and pulled at his clothes. He shivered. The puncture wounds on his finger stabbed and burned, and William felt an irrational sense of foreboding.

"Did you find it?" Sandra's slim figure was framed in the light of the front door as she called out to him.

"Yes, I'll be right there." William looked around again. The setting was peaceful and serene, and as normal as any suburban street could be in the darkness of a Wednesday evening. Feeling silly, he was about to go inside when he suddenly heard the whispering sound again and the fine hairs on the back of his neck stood on end.

Quickly, without looking behind him, he hurried up the path to the house and shut the door, locking it carefully as he did so.

5

*W*illiam walked with the locksmith to the door. "Thanks for coming so quickly. I want to use the basement for storing equipment while we carry out the renovations. We haven't had a chance to look down there yet. It was locked when we bought the house, darn estate agent was supposed to sort it... you know what they're like."

The tradesman nodded.

"I guess it will be a good size area. These old houses all have large basements."

He stood in the doorway and brushed at the dust

CARRIE KING & CAROLINE CLARK

which covered the sleeves of his uniform. "There's lots of dust around. I suppose there is still a fair amount of construction going on in the area."

"Yes." William followed the locksmith out onto the step. "Most of the houses are complete now, but there are still some to be finished. The dust will die down once the last of the work is complete."

He frowned up at the gathering clouds.

"Looks like bad weather is coming. Thanks for your help. I'll let you get on your way."

"No problem at all." The man walked back to his car, and William turned to walk back inside the house.

"I've got a torch!" Sandra was standing in the entrance way. Her sleeves were rolled up, and a smudge of dirt lay across her nose. Her light brown hair was piled up in a messy ponytail on the top of her head so she looked about 12 years old.

William felt a sudden burst of love.

"Look at you! You're so excited to see an old basement," William teased. He smiled indulgently at his wife. "The thought of lost treasure has lured you away but how's the cleaning going?"

The couple walked up the short corridor toward the basement door. A smile lit up her beautiful face and crinkled her eyes.

"I've finished washing down the shelves in the kitchen, and I'm about to start unpacking the boxes to put everything away. I can't believe the amount of dust everywhere! And as soon as I clean it away, more dust seems to fall and settle. I don't even know where it's all coming from."

"Yes, it is a little peculiar. But I'm sure it will stop soon." William placed his hand on the basement door handle and twinkled his eyes at his wife.

"Are you ready for whatever treasures we may find?"

Sandra switched on the torch.

"Aye, aye, sir. Lead the way forwards into our intrepid adventure!"

William laughed. "It's probably just a pile of old junk."

He flicked the switch at the top of the basement stairs, but the room below remained in darkness. He peered into the dim room, squinting his eyes, and flicked the switch up and down another few times.

"Looks like the bulb is out. Just as well you have that torch."

The couple walked carefully down the stairs. William felt a palpable chill as they moved downward, a damp and clammy feeling that tugged at him like an unwelcome embrace. He shivered involuntarily.

"Oh, what is that awful smell?" Sandra's voice was thick with distaste.

William could smell it too. He wrinkled his nose.

"It's something decaying. Perhaps a small animal crawled in here and died at some point. We don't know how long it's been since the room was opened up."

They'd reached the stone-tiled floor at the bottom of the flight of stairs. Sandra shone the torch around, the beam of light picked up several bulky shapes but showed very little around them.

"What is all of this?" she said, curiosity coloring her words with excitement.

William walked forward, looking around.

"Put the torch over here," he said as he pushed back a heavy tarpaulin and looked closely at the piece of equipment underneath.

"It's some kind of old fashioned laundry press. Looks industrial. How strange. I wonder why it's here?"

He dropped the tarpaulin, sending choking clouds of dust up in the air. He sneezed and stepped backward.

"I'll replace the bulb in the light at some stage and we'll look at everything more closely then. It's probably just rubbish. I think we'll find that it all just needs to be taken to the tip." He gazed around. "There's plenty of room down here for what we need."

Sandra sneezed as well, once, then twice.

"I'm not sure whether it's the awful smell or the dust that's making me sneeze. Oh!"

Sandra dropped the torch suddenly and it rolled across the flagstones, its beam making an arch across the far wall. She grabbed William's arm.

"What is it?" William said quickly. He felt jumpy and on edge himself which was ridiculous.

CARRIE KING & CAROLINE CLARK

"Oh, it was nothing. Sorry. I'm all jittery. I walked back into something and it gave me a fright."

Sandra giggled nervously. She let go of his arm and stooped to pick up the torch, turning to shine it behind her.

"It must be more of that equipment."

She shone the torch over several more of the dusty tarpaulins. "I don't like it down here, William. Let's go back upstairs."

As she spoke, the door at the top of the stairs flew shut with a bang. Sandra shrieked, and William felt his stomach drop down into his boots.

"The door must have caught a breeze and blown shut," he said, attempting to make his voice sound steady and reassuring, and yet failing dismally.

"Come on. Let's go. I'll sort this room out another day."

They hurried back up the stairs, and William was relieved when the door handle turned easily. He pulled the door open and they walked back into the light of the hallway. A cool breeze wrapped itself around his ankles as he closed the basement door again.

"Oh, that was spooky."

Sandra leaned into him. He enjoyed the sensation of her body pressed against his.

"I don't think I want to go down there again."

"It's just a cellar silly," he said as a shiver ran down his spine, what was wrong with him?

"Hello? Is there anyone there?" A woman's voice called from the entrance way.

Sandra and William exchanged glances and hurried back down the hallway. A young couple stood framed in the open front door, smiling broadly at them.

"Hello," said the young woman again. She looked from Sandra to William, and her gaze lingered for a moment. Her long blonde hair hung around her shoulders, and she was wearing a tight pink T-shirt and a tiny pair of jean shorts.

William's eyes flickered over her long, tanned legs.

"Sorry to disturb you. The door was open, and we thought we'd come over and introduce ourselves. I'm Lisa, and this is my husband Mike." She indicated the good-looking man standing beside her. "We're your neighbors."

"Oh, you're not disturbing us! We were just looking around the cellar." Sandra switched off the torch and beamed at the couple. "I'm Sandra, and this is my husband William."

"Nice to meet you."

William stepped forward and shook Mike's hand. The other man squeezed his hand just a little too tightly, in a short display of dominance.

"You've got a good grip there, Mike." William released Mike's hand and, as he did so, he felt the spider bite on the end of his finger tingle. He turned to the young woman.

"And it's nice to meet you too, Lisa."

She looked directly into his eyes, saying nothing, and a slight smile played across her lips. He felt an uncomfortable stirring as his body reacted to her obvious look, and in order to hide it he turned quickly to Sandra.

"My wife was about to make us a cup of coffee, weren't you, darling? Would you like to join us?"

"Oh, yes, I was," Sandra said. "And please do. I'm so happy you came over to introduce yourselves." She beamed at their new neighbors and led the way into the kitchen.

Lisa stepped forward to follow. She looked into William's eyes as she passed him, and he cleared his throat slightly, watching the pert jiggle of her barely-clothed, golden-tanned buttocks. As she swayed past, her shoulder brushed lightly against him.

"Well, how about you show me the house and grounds while the womenfolk make the refreshments?" Mike said heartily, his voice loud and slightly echoing.

He slapped a heavy hand on William's back.

William turned away from the kitchen, glad of the being led away from Lisa. This was not like him and it made him feel both uncomfortable and guilty.

"Sure. Maybe you can give me a hand to get the old pump working? I was looking at it earlier. I think with a bit of extra manpower we can get it going again."

6

William stood on a stepladder, clippers in hand. The lower branches of the sycamore trees needed trimming back, as they were blocking the sunlight from reaching the kitchen windows. He'd promised Sandra he'd finish the job today. With great satisfaction he snipped at the branches, watching as they fell to the ground.

"William?"

Sandra called his name from behind him.

He turned around to see her standing by the back door, her handbag slung over her arm.

"I'm going down to the shops. Do you need anything?"

"Maybe get some more bottles of that red wine? The one we had a few nights ago?"

Sandra nodded.

"I'll look for it."

She blew him a kiss and turned away.

William turned back to trimming the trees. As he cut through the last of the branches he heard her car start and pull away. Admiring his work he backed down the ladder. With that done, the kitchen would be much lighter and they would be able to see more of their neighbors.

"Hello there."

The voice behind him was low and seductive.

William whirled around to see Lisa standing just a few feet behind him, dressed in tight jeans and a short top which exposed her tanned midriff. He looked behind her, expecting to see Mike, but she was alone.

"Sandra has just left," he said quickly. "She should only be gone for an hour or two. Perhaps you can come back later?"

He felt uncomfortable being alone with this woman, with her too-direct stares and her confident self-awareness.

Lisa flicked her hair back over her shoulder and fixed him with one of her smoldering looks.

"I didn't come to see Sandra," she murmured.

William cleared his throat and quickly folded up the stepladder, holding it in front of him like a shield. "Can I help you with anything? It'll have to be quick, I have work to finish before Sandra gets back."

Lisa lowered her long, thick lashes for a moment, then looked up from under them.

"Mike was telling me that you said there was an old laundry press in your cellar. I was wondering if I could see it? I've been studying the history of Briar Park. Your house is the original homestead, and at one point the house was used as an institution. I thought I could take some photos of the old equipment. I'm thinking of putting together some kind of scrapbook."

William felt a spike of interest.

"The house certainly has quite a past. We didn't find out much about the previous owners or why it's been empty so long. Maybe we can find something exciting out."

Shifting the ladders to his side, he pointed at the house.

"You can take a look at the presses if you like... I've been planning to take them to the tip. They're of no use to us."

He walked over to the house, leaning the stepladder against the peeling wooden boards and placing the clippers down on the small veranda. He glanced over at Lisa, who now stood beside him.

"I wouldn't have picked you as a historian."

Lisa looked at him, holding his gaze a little too long and a little too directly. For a moment he felt uncomfortable.

"I think you'll be surprised once you discover all my talents," she said softly.

William felt a rush of blood to his head. His cheeks burned. Flustered, he looked away for a moment to compose himself.

"Where is Mike today?" he asked quickly.

Lisa shrugged her shapely shoulders. Her brief top rose up even higher. William saw the flash of a diamante navel ring against her tanned skin.

"He's out," she said dismissively.

William looked at Lisa's empty hands. "I thought you said you wanted to take a photo of the laundry presses? Do you have a camera?"

"Not here with me. Perhaps I can have a look first?"

William felt uneasy. He looked around but there was nothing to help him.

At the edge of the property the leaves of the now trimmed sycamore tree rustled. Beneath them, a yellow cloud of dust twirled and then spun across the yard.

"I can give you just a quick look, then I'd better get

back to work. I've got a lot of chores to do, and Sandra will be back soon."

He hated how he sounded like a guilty child and wished he could turn her away, but somehow it didn't seem right. So he led the way inside and stopped in front of the cellar door.

"I fixed the bulb a few days ago. It is still quite dim down here though, so do watch your step."

Lisa moved close up behind him as he pushed the door open. For a second he thought he felt her full breasts press against his back, and then the pressure moved away. Flustered, he hurried down the stairs, anxious to put some space between himself and the pushy woman. He reached the flagstone floor and looked back as Lisa made her way down the stairs, her bosom moving up and down as she seemed to bounce down the steps.

Clearing his throat, William pulled back the tarpaulin covering the press. A billow of choking dust enveloped him and he waved his hands in front of his face to clear it.

"This damned dust."

He dropped the tarpaulin to the floor and turned around.

"Lisa?"

The basement behind him was empty.

William frowned. Had she gone back upstairs? What was the woman up to? He coughed slightly as the dust continued to swirl in the air in front of his face.

"Lisa?"

"I'm here," her voice was low and soft.

Frowning, William stepped behind the press, toward the sound of her voice. He gasped. Lisa was standing by the basement wall. She had removed her top and her full, tanned breasts were bare. As he watched, she dropped her top to the floor, never removing her eyes from his.

"What are you doing? Put that back on... I think you should leave," William spluttered out the words and took a step backward. He glanced wildly toward the stairs looking for a way to escape.

A whispering noise began, filling the basement, and quickly intensifying. It wrapped itself around his head and squeezed tightly. Confused, he spun around to find the source as the spider bite on his finger throbbed and ached.

"Come to me," Lisa said, her voice a soft caress, rose above the whispers. She lifted her arms and held them out toward him in an enticing gesture.

William shook his head to try and clear it of the whispering which seemed to support her, to lead to her, to surround her. He could now make out some of the words through the heavy sibilant sound.

"*Gooo,*" the voice hissed. "*Go to heeeer. She can ssssshow you pleasuresssss you've never dreamed of. Go!*" It was an order.

"No!" The word escaped William's lips even as his feet involuntarily moved toward Lisa.

She stood against the wall, her eyes fixed on his as the whispers pushed him toward her. Teasing against his ear. Tantalizing him forward with mystery and intrigue. What did they mean, what did they promise?

Lisa stretched, arching her back and pushing her breasts towards him. William felt drawn to her and he could not look away. An irresistible force pulled him forward, and as he fought against it, he felt himself falling and spinning into her gaze.

"Toooouch her," the whispering voice filled his head, obliterating all rational thought. *"Touch her and lose yourself in dessssire."* The voice was insidious and provoking, taunting him.

"No!" William now stood directly in front of the woman, though he didn't remember moving there. He tried to pull himself back, forcing the image of Sandra to the front of his mind.

It was no use, he was drowning in Lisa's eyes, their depths eternal and overwhelmingly attractive. Helplessly, he felt his body react to her.

"Come to me."

Lisa placed her hands on William's ribcage, the heat of her skin burning through his clothes. Her lips parted, and she darted a small pink tongue across the soft skin of her lower lip. Her eyes held promises beyond anything he had ever imagined. She ran her fingers down his body and around to his back, inching lower until her hands gripped his buttocks.

"Come to me."

William was dimly aware of a low, evil cackling which echoed around the cellar mixing with the sibilant hiss of the whispers.

Lisa reached down and began to undo the zipper of his jeans.

7

*T*hree weeks later

Sandra stared at herself in the bathroom mirror. Her face was white, and her eyes looked huge against her pale skin. Her lower lip trembled as she gazed at her reflection.

As she watched, a single tear dropped from the corner of one eye and rolled down her face. She wiped it away, leaving a faint smear on her skin. Her heart hurt. She could physically feel the pain. William had never spoken to her like that before.

"Sandra?" William's voice called up the stairs, heavy with impatience. "What are you doing? I need your help with this. Why must you always be so exasperating?"

Sandra swallowed hard, trying to compose herself. She had no idea what had gotten into her husband, but over the past few weeks his personality had changed dramatically. He was mean, sarcastic, and impatient. She had never seen this side of him before, and she did not like it one bit.

"Sandra!" William shouted her name again. "Come here!"

She jumped, afraid of the tone she could hear in his voice. She already knew that if she went to him he would talk to her harshly and cruelly, tell her she was stupid, and make her feel bad about herself.

She sniffed and took a deep breath before walking to the top of the stairs and peering over.

She looked down to where William was holding one end of the laundry press, part of it out the door and part of it still sitting on the floorboards of the entrance way.

"I don't think I can help you anymore," she said finally having the courage to stand up for herself.

"You keep telling me that I'm not doing it right. And anyway, it's far too heavy for me. Do you want me to go and ask Mike?"

"Do you want me to go and ask Mike?" William mimicked her, his voice heavy with contempt. "No, I don't want you to go and ask Mike. I need you to get your useless arse down here and give me a hand."

Sandra swallowed hard.

"No," she said firmly. "I will not help you if you continue to talk to me like that."

"Oh, for Christ's sake."

William dropped his hands from the press and turned away.

"You useless bitch," he muttered under his breath, before pushing past the piece of equipment and stomping out the front door.

Sandra sank down onto the top stair and dropped her head into her hands. The pain and confusion in her heart threatened to overwhelm her. What had happened to their wonderful marriage? They'd been so happy. But, seemingly overnight, William had changed, and she was at a complete loss as to what could have caused such a drastic turn-about in his personality.

The bathroom door suddenly slammed behind her and Sandra jumped. She frowned. She was sure that there were no windows open upstairs, but surely it had been a breeze that had caused the door to slam. She felt a ripple of cold fingers run up her spine and she shivered, pushing herself to her feet. She opened the bathroom door and looked inside. The window remained firmly closed.

As she stood in the doorway, a low whispering swirled around her head. She turned quickly. On the landing, a cloud of yellow dust swirled, spinning like a small tornado in front of her. As Sandra watched, it dissolved and dispersed, leaving a sprinkling of dust across the dark floorboards.

As she stared at the dust she heard voices downstairs. With a deep trepidation, she leaned over the banister rail to look down.

William had returned with Mike, and within moments, the men had hoisted the laundry press up and carried it outside.

Sandra sighed and turned back to the bathroom. She

walked in and turned on the taps, rinsing her hands in the cool water. She looked up to study her reflection again, and jumped in surprise. Someone was standing behind her shoulder.

Sandra whirled around, but there was no one there. Her heart beat rapidly against her chest as she turned back to the mirror. No, she had not imagined it; there it was again.

The face of a young nun was looking back at her from over her left shoulder. "I will help if I can, this has to end," the words were in her head, little more than a whisper.

As Sandra watched, the woman stared sadly at her for several seconds. Then her hand went to the silver cross at her neck before the image shimmered and disappeared.

She felt lightheaded and disoriented.

Shaking her head to try and clear it, Sandra turned off the tap and reached for a hand towel. A faint smell of sulfur reached her nostrils, stinging and penetrating. She could hear the men moving about downstairs, taking another piece of equipment from the cellar to the trailer that William had hired to transport the junk to the tip. She suddenly felt exhausted, barely able to keep her eyes open. Dropping the towel to the floor, she stumbled across the landing and fell across the bed.

SANDRA'S EYES SNAPPED OPEN. The room was dark. Outside, she could hear the wind howling, rattling at the windows and shaking the tiles on the roof.

She jumped as she felt something touch her foot, and quickly she scrambled upright, struggling to see in the gloom.

"William?" her voice was shaky in the darkness.

"Lazy bitch," William's voice was cold and hard.

She heard him move around to his side of the bed.

"You slept the whole afternoon away while I tidied the basement."

She heard the sound of his belt buckle and the soft sigh of his zipper. His pants hit the floor with a muffled thud, and the side of the bed suddenly dipped as he put his weight on it. He reached for her with rough hands that dug into her shoulder.

"You can make yourself useful to me now," he said.

Sandra pushed at him.

"What are you doing? You're hurting me." Her fingers scrabbled across the bare skin of his chest. "William, what has gotten into you?" She pulled herself away and sat on the edge of the bed, breathing heavily. "What time is it?" She still felt disoriented and weak.

William suddenly grabbed her hair and yanked it, hard.

She screamed in pain.

"Let me go!"

He pulled her backward onto the bed next to him and then threw himself on top of her, straddling her with his legs.

Sandra pushed and struggled, feeling tiny pieces of his skin catching under her nails.

William grabbed her wrists and flung them over her head, holding them down on the mattress.

"Stay still," he ordered.

The whispering started again, filling the room with its rapid rustle and hiss.

Sandra whipped her head wildly from one side to the other. "Let me go!" she shouted, lifting her hips to try and fling William off her.

William bent his head suddenly and bit hard at her neck. The pain rushed up to her head in a sharp torrent of agony. She screamed and struggled harder.

"Get off me!"

The whispering around her intensified, almost manic in its tone and urgency as it urged him on.

Suddenly, William's weight lifted and Sandra was free. She threw herself off the bed and stood to one side, breathing heavily.

"Don't. You. Ever. Do. That. Again," she said as she fought to control her breathing. Heart pounding, she turned around and switched on the bedroom light, putting her hand up to the bite mark on her neck as she did so. It came away covered in blood.

She looked back into the room. William was lying

back on the bed, naked except for the sheet covering his groin. There was something malevolent about the gaze on his face. His hand moved rapidly up and down beneath the sheet. A slow, nasty smile played over his lips as he leered at her.

A dark whispering filled every corner of the bedroom. Rising to such a frenzy that it was like a physical presence pushing and pulling at her.

Sandra turned away in disgust. "What are you doing? How are you making that noise? And why did you do that to me? I don't even know who you are anymore!"

She ran out of the bedroom and down the stairs, tears falling from her eyes as the whispers followed her down the stairs. Salt and fire were two words that she could make out, but the rest of it was just a sound. It raked across the hairs on her neck and turned her stomach over.

8

*S*andra walked downstairs heavily, carrying her travel bag. Her shoulders drooped, and she felt old beyond her years. Never could she ever have imagined that the day would come when she would leave William. But she knew in her heart that she wasn't leaving the William she'd fallen in love with. The man who now shared her house was not the man she had married. Something had changed and a darkness had fallen on him since they came to the house in Briar Park.

She reached the bottom of the stairs and placed the bag on the floorboards. She'd spent last night on the couch in the living room, and her neck ached where William had bitten her. She had no idea where he was now. She had not seen him this morning, and he had not shown his face while she packed her things.

Quickly, she looked into the kitchen. Despite her anger, she could not leave without speaking to him. The kitchen was empty. She walked over to the far wall and peered out of the window at the garden, her hands grazing the yellow dust which covered the sill.

There he was.... digging in the vegetable patch, his back to her.

Sandra looked around the room, her eyes filling with tears. She'd felt so happy when they'd moved in here, sure that they would spend the rest of their days in this house. She'd been so sure that they would soon have children and that she and William would grow old together. And now everything had changed. Sighing, she walked along the short corridor to the back door and placed her hand on the door handle. It didn't move under her touch. Frowning, she pulled at the door. Was it locked?

She pressed her face up to the small window in the door and called to William. He did not turn around.

Irritated, Sandra walked through the house to the front door. As she stepped into the entrance way, a swirl of yellow dust spun through the air and into the living room. She knew for sure that she wouldn't miss all the dust.

She tried to open the front door, but that too was locked. William always left keys in the door, but there was nothing hanging from the lock. She walked back into the kitchen, searching. She was becoming angry now. Had William locked her inside on purpose?

The keys were nowhere to be seen. Sandra pulled open drawers and searched through the cupboards, growing crosser by the minute. This was ridiculous! She fumbled with the window latch, determined to open the window and shout at William to come and let her out.

The window would not budge.

Sandra dropped the latch and banged her open palms against the glass, shouting William's name. He either did not hear her, or he was ignoring her as he continued his digging out in the garden.

The low whispering began again, rushing through the kitchen and slamming into Sandra's ears like a sharp slap.

She looked around frantically, trying to find the source of the noise. She suddenly heard the back door open and she ran out of the kitchen. William was walking toward her, the bulk of his body blocking the hallway.

"Why did you lock me in?" she shouted at him. "Let me out now, or I'll call the police."

William frowned at her. He lifted one hand, the skin covered with crumbs of wet earth, and reached out as if to stroke her hair. "Sandra ...?" he sounded distant and puzzled.

Sandra ducked her head, moving out of his reach. "Don't touch me," she hissed. "Don't ever touch me again."

William shook his head, as if trying to shake away an annoying bug. He looked at her, but his eyes were cloudy and unfocused. "What is the matter, darling?"

Sandra snatched up her travel bag and pushed past him, hurrying toward the back door. "You're mad. I'm leaving."

She wrenched at the door, but it was locked again,

the key nowhere in sight. In a rage, she turned back, shouting at her husband, "Unlock the door and let me out!"

"I'm sorry, Sandra." William's tone of voice was almost musical. He had the same faraway look in his eye. "I couldn't help myself. She made me do it."

"What are you talking about?" Sandra dropped the suitcase on the floor at her feet and held out her hand. "Give me the key." Her voice was shaking.

William took a step toward her.

"Stay there!" she warned. "Just give me the key, and I'll leave."

William stood in one spot, swaying gently. He shook his head again, a frown wrinkling his brow. "The whispers ...," he said.

Sandra stared at him. "Have you heard them too? They are infuriating. I thought you had something to do with the noise. That it was you making me hear things..."

"The whispers. I can't stop myself doing what they tell me to do."

He looked at her sadly, and for a moment Sandra caught a glimpse of the old William in his tortured gaze.

"The whispers enticed me and called me, and they told me to do it."

"Made you do what?"

Sandra looked around wildly. She was starting to feel claustrophobic with the door behind her and William's body blocking her path out of the narrow hallway.

"William, can you get out of the way?"

"They made me have sex with Lisa." William's voice was almost a moan. His shoulders drooped.

"What?" Sandra stared at her husband in horror. "You've got to be kidding me. Lisa, our neighbor? When did this happen? Who made you do it? What are you talking about?"

He continued speaking, as if she'd said nothing. "Lisa is pregnant."

9

*S*andra stood in the kitchen, breathing heavily. Her entire world had been ripped away from her, and everything she thought she knew had collapsed. And still she couldn't get out of this damned house!

Afraid, weak-kneed, she glared at William.

He was now sitting at the kitchen table, his head in his hands.

"Don't sit there feeling sorry for yourself. No one could have forced you to do that." She wanted to hit him, to scream, to rip his eyes from his face. "You disgust me," she shouted, her voice dripped with loathing.

William said nothing.

Sandra turned away and rattled the window latch again. "Why can't I open any of the windows or doors? I need to leave, William. Let me out now or I'm going to call the locksmith."

She reached for the phone and held it to her ear. There was no dial tone. Angrily, Sandra stabbed at the disconnect button over and over, but still there was no tone. She slammed the phone back down onto the cradle.

"And the phone is dead! What is going on?"

She rushed out of the kitchen again, grabbing at the front door handle with both hands and pulling at it frantically, but it was all to no avail. She turned back to the kitchen and gasped.

Standing in front of her was the shadowy figure of a young nun. She reached out a hand towards Sandra, her shape fading in and out of view.

"The time is now."

"What!" Sandra shouted, but the words were gone and so was the nun. Yet somehow she felt better. More relaxed than she had in weeks. It was like being in the presence of a parent after a nightmare. Somehow you knew that now you were safe.

The nun reappeared, her eyes sad and full of tears.

"Run! Run while you still can!" the young woman whispered and she held onto her silver cross. "Go quickly with God."

Sandra screamed and William, finally roused from his stupor, ran from the kitchen.

"What? What is it?"

Sandra stared at the empty space where the nun had stood just moments ago. "There was someone here."

William looked around. His eyes were no longer glassy. He seemed alert and fully conscious. "Can you smell that?" he said suddenly.

Sandra sniffed the air. The faint, acrid smell of smoke reached her. "Something is on fire."

They both looked down the hallway toward the back door. A curl of black smoke wove its way out from under the door to the basement and hovered in the corridor. "The house is on fire! William, you have to get us out! Smash a window!"

10

Sandra ran after William as he rushed back into the kitchen. He picked up one of the wooden chairs and lobbed it at the window pane. The chair bounced back into the room, not making a scratch on the glass. Sandra screamed and picked up the electric kettle, throwing it at the window and screaming again when it bounced off uselessly, leaving the glass intact.

"William," she shouted hysterically as smoke began to fill the room, "We're trapped!"

The nun was back, walking into the kitchen she went to the cupboard and pulled out a bag of salt.

Sandra felt better seeing her there and yet she

couldn't explain it. She reached out and felt William take her hand.

The nun looked at a pile of tea towels and pointed at the tap. Sandra didn't understand and she could feel the heat rising in the house and the flames whipped up and raged toward them.

"Wet them," William said and ran to the sink.

Quickly he dumped them into the sink and turned on the tap. As they were soaked with water he wrapped one around her mouth and put another over her head.

Sandra's eyes were filled with tears. This would not stop the flames. The nun was tipping salt on the window frame and then in front of the doors. Occasionally she would look at them and there were tears in her eyes.

"What are we to do?" Sandra asked.

"The cellar, maybe we can survive in there?"

Sandra nodded and helped him with the tea towels. Once they were all soaked they took each other's hand and headed for the cellar door.

The smoke was thick now and even with the tea towels over their mouths the smoke clogged their throat and threatened to block up their lungs. Flames leaped at them as they crossed the hallway.

William reached the door as they watched the nun spreading salt in front of the windows.

He grabbed the handle but the cellar door wouldn't open. The sound of roaring could be heard in the flames and a wind blew the blaze toward them.

Sandra dropped to her knees, scalded and choking but the door wouldn't open. They would die here, together and it seemed so unfair.

Then the nun appeared before them. Like a breath of fresh air her presence cooled them and she put her hand over William's. Together they turned the handle and the door opened.

As a cool breeze came from the cellar it fanned the flames behind them and they were engulfed for a moment. Sandra could feel it blistering her skin but then a hand pushed her and she was stumbling down the stairs as the door was slammed shut behind her.

William stopped and packed wet towels against the door jamb before following her down into the cellar.

Together they huddled in the darkness wondering if they would make it out alive. Things were different. William was like himself and Sandra knew that something had taken hold of him. Something had used him and once it was done it had wanted to kill him. Had it lit the fire?

No, that was the nun and that was done to save them... or maybe to save the people who came after. She rested her head against William's chest and pulled the tea towel tight over her nose. Breathing in the damp but mostly smoke-free air.

The fire raged above and the heat was unbearable. They knew that it would be a race between life and death. The fire wanted to consume them but hopefully they would survive long enough for it to burn out.

As the smoke seeped into her lungs she fell into a deep sleep.

11

*S*everal fire engines stood outside the house, sirens wailing. Firemen in heavy uniforms dashed this way and that, spraying strong jets of water at the house in Briar Park.

Neighbors gathered on the street, watching the unfolding events with horror. Mike and Lisa stood at the entrance to their drive, the man's arm slung protectively around the shoulders of his young wife.

"We can contain it and stop it from spreading, but that's all," Bert, the fire chief, called to the young fireman standing beside him. He struggled to hold the squirming, writhing firehose as it pulsed torrents of water onto the flames.

"We're not going to be able to save the house."

"Was there anyone inside?" the young man shouted back.

"The neighbors seem to think that the owners were there. God save their souls," answered Bert.

He stared into the hypnotic glare of the fire. The stench of burning plastic and rubber filled the air and his eyes watered. No, there was no way anyone could still be alive in that hellish mess.

Some hours later the last remaining smoke curled up from the property and then part of the floor gave way.

Bert stood and surveyed the smoldering ruins, his heart heavy. No matter how many fires he attended, it still wrenched at his heartstrings to see someone's hopes and dreams destroyed like this. Especially when there were fatalities involved.

Exhausted men rushed forward as they heard a scream.

They splayed torches across the ruins and then they could see an opening into the cellar and something was moving in the depths of the house.

Quickly the men lowered a ladder down into the wreckage and before long they were carrying out the still forms of two people.

"They're alive," one of the men called and Bert let out a sigh of joy.

This was a good day. To find someone in that wreckage was a miracle and as he moved across the wreckage he saw something shine in the embers before him. He kicked at it with his foot to reveal a silver cross in amongst the burnt wood and rubble. It looked new, untouched by the flames and he picked it up.

"Sandra," a weak voice called.

"Here my love," came the reply.

Bert saw the hand of a young woman reaching out and he walked over and put the cross into her fingers. She was covered in smoke and soot but looked remarkably well. For a moment their eyes met and she nodded as her fingers gripped onto the cross.

Bert glanced at the ambulance as the two survivors were loaded aboard. It was emblazoned with emergency colors and the hospital's crest. As he watched, the doors were closed and the vehicle whisked away two of the luckiest people he knew.

He'd make a few notes, then he would head back to the station. Once everything had cooled down it would be the turn of forensics to sift through the wreckage for anything that could indicate the cause of the fire.

Bert stood to one side of the ruins of the house as he wrote in his notepad. He was suddenly aware of a low whispering sound and he looked up, cocking his head to one side. The back of his neck prickled. It was an unpleasant sound—but what was causing it? He glanced over to the scorched trunks of the sycamore trees, hardly more than blackened stumps now, their scorched leaves remained and seemed to be making such a sound.

EPILOGUE

*I*n a room in the hospital two people were ready to be signed off from the burns unit. Even though they had been below the raging fire they had come away relatively unscathed.

William and Sandra had stayed in the hospital for a month and had since been visiting regularly for the next seven months. Now they were finally being discharged and were ready to start again with their own lives.

As they walked out, they took each other's hand and walked along the corridors.

"Coffee?" William asked.

Sandra nodded and they walked along the corridor and into the café.

While Sandra took a seat, William got them two drinks and came over.

"Do you remember anything yet," she asked as he set the drinks down and pulled out a seat opposite her.

William sat down and hutched the chair in. "Nothing but the whispering. It was all I could think of and it seemed to tell me what to do. It seemed to rule me."

"Sometimes I wonder if you just pretend to forget," Sandra said. "If you ever cheat again we are over."

"I know and I love you too much to risk such a thing."

"You'd better," she said.

Then she thought back to that time and she too remembered the whispering. The way it made her feel and the way it raised the hair on her neck. Then she thought of the nun. William said he didn't remember her but she knew that was a lie. She thought he just didn't believe it had really happened.

That he thought it was just a hallucination, or something they had imagined to get them through. Only she knew it was real. That the nun had helped them escape.

Sandra had asked if the nun had been found and was told that no one else was in the house. That was when she had looked into the history of the house and when she found out about Sister Agnes and how she died there.

Though it made no sense, she knew that the sister had saved them and that she had made sure that the evil in Briar Park was trapped within its walls as it burned. She knew that it was over and with the insurance money they could start again.

Then she decided if they ever had a girl she would call her Agnes.

"Thank you," the words were whispered in her ear.

IN THE MATERNITY ward of the same hospital a woman screamed.

"One more push. You can do it," the midwife said briskly, staring intently between Lisa's legs.

"Your baby is nearly here."

Moments later the slippery baby sped into the world, and Lisa fell back against the pillows, exhausted.

Mike mopped her sweat-soaked forehead and smiled at her encouragingly. "You did it!"

The couple looked over toward where the midwife stood at one side of the room, her back now to them.

"Is the baby all right? Is it a boy or a girl?" Lisa called out anxiously.

The midwife looked down, her face pulled into a mask of sadness and sorrow. She swallowed hard. Despite her years of experience, she had to stop herself from dropping the baby and crying out in disgust and fear.

The little boy squirmed in her arms, covered in the gore of birth, as he opened his tiny mouth in a silent and distorted scream.

But instead of the cherubic face of a newborn, the

face that looked up at her was twisted and deformed, its eyes red and inflamed, its nose no more than a snout, and its contorted mouth pulled into a perpetual and permanent sneer ...

THE END

SOMETHING EVIL THIS WAY COMES
– PREVIEW

Did you miss the first book in this series? Grab it now for 0.99 or FREE on KU Something Evil This Way Comes or read on for a hair-raising preview:

Brother Thomas bent over his work, the quill dancing elegantly over the page was making inky cursive loops on the paper as he scratched the point of the feather across the surface. For a moment he stopped and ran a hand through his thick black hair. All the monks kept their hair short and without style. Such things were mere distractions and Thomas knew, that as usual, his hair was too long.

It didn't seem to matter how often he cut it, it would grow and soon he would be receiving disapproving looks. Deciding to cut it tomorrow he went back to copying the text.

It was a beautiful book but complicated in places. The message was one of hope and it inspired him as he wrote. Deep in concentration, he did not hear the scrape and scrabble of claws on the stone floor behind him. So busy was he that he failed to notice the sudden deathly drop in temperature, and the stench of rotten meat that pervaded the air. None of this crossed his mind until it was too late.

The creature sprang from where it was crouched in the shadows, a terrifying blur of teeth and scaly limbs, and fixed itself to Brother Thomas' back.

Agony opened his mouth to form a scream, and his hands flew to his throat in an attempt to claw away the excruciating pain. His scream was cut off before it even began, dying to a gurgle as the creature's talons sliced through his voice box and a stream of hot blood gushed forth. The last thing Brother Thomas' horrified gaze glimpsed was the sight of a pair of evil yellow eyes peering intently into his own. Pain seared through him as well as fear and disbelief. Holding onto his faith he gratefully surged forward to meet his Maker. With one last gurgle, the monk's eyes rolled back in his head and his body fell heavily to the ground.

Viciously, the creature dragged its claws across Brother Thomas' face, laying his flesh wide open. It leaned forward and sniffed deeply at the scent of fresh blood. Crouched over the monk's body, it was a horrible and hellish sight. Scabby dun-colored skin covered a bony body, and the ribcage and shoulder blades were clearly visible through the thin, parchment-like covering. Long black talons protruded evilly from each curled paw. Two dark, horn-like bumps poked up from above its heavy brows. The mouth was wide, rimmed with sharp yellow fangs, and a long drop of drool hung from one tooth.

The creature hooked its claws into the monk's shoulders and proceeded to drag his body away, into the shadows, a trail of blood glistening on the flagstones as it pulled the monk into the gloom of an alcove. The small room was soon filled with the dreadful sound of ripping flesh, gnashing teeth, and dripping blood.

Brother Luke balanced the boxes of beeswax candles in his arms and strode along the corridor towards the kitchen. His stomach was rumbling, and he hoped that he might find something to eat. Some cheese, a slice of cold meat, or an apple, perhaps. His mouth watered at the thought.

A tinge of guilt came and went. Yes, he'd eaten more than his share at lunchtime, and he had both seen and felt Father Matthew's frown as he'd helped himself to his third bowl of soup, but he was a big boy. He needed a little extra. Sure, some might look at his swelling belly and traces of a double chin with slight condemnation, but he did enjoy his food and didn't like to restrict himself. At the thought of some tasty morsel he licked his lips in anticipation.

A sudden noise, a frenzied whispering, reached his ears and the hairs on the back of his neck stood on end. What was that unholy sound? Stopping mid-stride, he looked behind him. The corridor was bare, except for... he squinted his eyes. Was that a movement?

Something unseen and hidden was scrabbling in the shadows?

"Who is there?" he called, his voice slightly unsteady as his heart pounded in his chest. The sound of his voice echoed in the empty corridor.

Brother Luke waited, breath held, trying to hear over the blood that rushed through his ears. Every inch of his body told him something was wrong and yet his mind rejected such a thought.

The whispering grew louder.

Tendrils of fear curled around him like a vine. Deciding he didn't want to find out what was there, he turned and hurried on his way, towards the warmth and safety of the kitchen.

A sudden chill crept into the room and curled around Brother Ian's ankles. Shaking off a shiver, he pulled his cloak closer around him. Being thin and a little older meant that he always felt the cold, though he should be used to it by now. Ian had been at the monastery since he was a boy of five.

The candle on his desk flickered and died before springing back to life. Brother Ian started and then sniffed the air, at the sudden distasteful smell. Where was it coming from? The same place as the chill? He looked around, uneasy. Something didn't feel right. Quickly, he crossed himself and murmured a short prayer.

Placing both feet firmly on the ground, he climbed down from his high stool and stood beside the desk for a moment. His room was stark, as each of the monk's living quarters were, a tiny space with just a narrow bed, a cupboard for his few clothes, high desk and stool, and a large wooden cross hanging from the wall. Brother Ian glanced at the cross and then quickly looked back again, frowning. Somehow the decoration had fallen and pivoted and was now hanging upside down from its hook.

Heart pounding at such an omen, Brother Ian hitched up his cloak and removed his sandals. Climbing on top of the thin bed covering, he reached up and righted the cross, once again whispering a prayer. Something, a breath of wind or a premonition, scudded across the back of his neck. Shivering again and unable to quell the heavy sense of dread, he climbed back off the bed and replaced his sandals. For just a moment he was transported to his childhood, and he was sure that something was about to reach from under the bed and snatch at his ankles. Shaking his head to clear the thought, he picked up the candle from his desk and pulled open the heavy wooden door. He would go and find one of his brothers. He had clearly spent too much time alone.

Father Matthew pushed his rimless glasses back on his head and sighed. Raising his hands he rubbed at his eyes, he had been reading far too long, and they ached. Carefully he marked his place and closed the heavy tome and then scratched his bald head. Though he had lost his hair some twenty years ago, sometimes it still surprised him. *Who wouldn't lose their hair looking after all these monks?* He chuckled to himself remembering some of the incidents over the years, though sometimes the memories were harder to find these last few months.

The candles in the sconces in the wall flickered and darkened, and he glanced towards the door, expecting to see it standing open and allowing a draught to flood into the room. The door remained firmly closed. A sudden chill, and an uncomfortable feeling inched its way up his spine. He shrugged his shoulders and wiggled on his seat. He needed to move about. It did a man of his age no good at all to sit for so long.

"Father Matthew!"

The door banged back on its hinges, slamming into the stone wall.

Grab Something Evil This Way Comes on Amazon just 0.99 or FREE on KU

ALSO BY CARRIE KING

Other Books Available

To be the first to hear about books from Carrie King and
Caroline Clark join Caroline's newsletter at CazClark.com

Briar Park Books:

Something Evil This Way Comes

With Wicked Intent

Silent Screaming

The Darkness in the Shadow

**If you can't wait for my next book why not grab
one of Caroline's:**

The Ghosts of RedRise House 4 book box set

Includes:

The Sacrifice - Dark things happened in RedRise House.
Acts so bad they left a stain on the soul of the building.
Now something is lurking there... waiting... dare you enter
this most haunted house?

The Battle Within - The Ghosts of RedRise House have escaped. Something evil is stalking the city and only Rosie stands between it and a chain of misery and death.

Suffer the Children – Two young ghost hunters find themselves in a house that will not let them leave.

Still Evil - Something has returned to the house and it wants blood. Two children are missing and alone. When they are found they think they are safe, but are they? RedRise House has something more to give. Can an old friend come back to save the day once more? How much will he need to give up and is this too much to ask?

Grab The Ghosts of RedRise House Box Set Now FREE on KINDLE UNLIMITED – the ghosts are only children how dangerous can they be?

Standalone Books

The Haunting of Brynlee House Based on a real haunted house - Brynlee House has a past, a secret, it is one that would be best left buried.

The Haunting of Shadow Hill House A move for a better future becomes a race against the past. Something dark lurks in Shadow Hill House and it is waiting.

Daddy Won't Kill You A rocking chair, relaxing, comfortable, soaked in the blood of its victims. – Based on a true story about The Dead Man's Chair

The Spirit Guide Series:

The Haunting of Seafield House - Gail wants to create some memories – if she survives the night in Seafield House it is something she will never forget.

The Haunting on the Hillside - Called From Beyond – The Spirit Guide - A Woman in White Ghost Story. A non-believer, a terrible accident, a stupid mistake. Is Mark going mad or was his girlfriend Called from Beyond?

The Haunting of Oldfield Drive - DarkMan Alone in the dark, Margie must face unimaginable terror. Is this thing that haunts her nights a ghost or is it something worse?

©COPYRIGHT 2018 CARRIE KING

All Rights Reserved
Carrie King

License Notes
This e-Book is licensed for personal enjoyment only.
It may not be resold or given away to others. If you
wish to share this book, please purchase an
additional copy. If you are reading this book and it
was not purchased then, you should purchase your
own copy. Your continued respect for author's rights
is appreciated.

©COPYRIGHT 2018 CARRIE KING

This story is a work of fiction any resemblance to people is purely coincidence. All places, names, events, businesses, etc. are used in a fictional manner. All characters are from the imagination of the author.

30448721R00062

Made in the USA
Columbia, SC
27 October 2018